CMS

Miriam Young

BEWARE THE POLAR BEAR!

Safety on the Ice

Illustrated by Robert Quackenbush

Lothrop, Lee & Shepard Co. · New York

Ever since Thanksgiving Scott had been thinking about ice skating.

"All we need is a few more cold nights," his father said, "and the pond will start to freeze. We'd better sharpen your ice skates, Scott."

"I want some skates," said Scott's little sister Mindy.

"We'll have to get some for you," Mrs. Benson said.

3

There was a skim of ice on the pond the next morning, but by noon it had melted in the sun. The following morning skim ice again covered the pond, making it look gray instead of blue. It was very cold that day, and the skim ice did not melt. Boys passing the pond on their way to the school bus threw stones from the road to see if they would sink. The stones held—even big ones. But Mr. Benson had to speak to the boys.

"If you like to skate, better not throw stones. If your skate hits one, you'll fall."

"OK, Mr. Benson," the boys said. "We were just trying to see how thick the ice was."

Mr. Benson said he would test the ice and tie a red cloth to a willow near the shore when it was safe.

On Friday morning Scott saw a big white dog that belonged to some new neighbors running across the ice. "Look at that, Mother. If it holds him it ought to hold me. He's as big as a polar bear!"

"Never mind," said Mrs. Benson. "I don't care if you see ten bears; don't step on the ice until your father tests it."

The next morning Mr. Benson cut a small hole in the ice near the edge. It was three inches thick. He put on his skates and went all over the lake, inspecting the ice. Then he tied a red cloth to the willow.

"OK, Scott. It's safe," he said when he came back.

"Yay!" Scott cheered. And he ran to telephone his friends. He told them he'd meet them on the ice. One friend, George, had already seen the red cloth.

Mindy wanted to go skating, too. "All right," Mrs. Benson said. "I'll take you to town with me and buy some skates for you today."

As Scott got into his jacket she added, "Watch out for cracks in the ice. When I was a girl in the city I used to skate in the park. My skate blade caught in a crack once, and I went right down and hit my head."

"Stay with the other kids," his father cautioned. "Don't go skating off alone. And keep away from dark spots, if you see any. Dark spots can mean thin ice."

Scott zipped up his jacket. What did they think he was, a baby like Mindy? "OK, OK," he said. "Cracks, dark spots, and stay with the others. Anything else?"

"And watch out for polar bears," Mindy said.

Scott laughed. He put his mittens in his pocket and tucked his skates under his arm. "All right, I've got it: spots and cracks, don't skate alone, and beware the polar bear. May I go now?"

Mr. and Mrs. Benson and Mindy went down to the edge of the pond with him.

Scott saw his friends, George and Andy, across the pond. "I hope I remember how to skate backward," he said as he laced up his hockey skates. He stood up and moved forward cautiously. "Hey, the ice is slipperier this year!"

"Remember what I taught you last year," his father said. "Lean forward and keep your knees bent and supple, like springs. Then if you start to fall, you can catch yourself."

Scott was getting used to the ice now. Waving to his family, he skated off.

Later that afternoon the Benson family went skating together. Mr. Benson had racing skates with long blades. Mrs. Benson had white figure skates. Mindy had her new double runners. Mr. Benson taught Scott a few tricks, while Mrs. Benson helped Mindy. It was her first time on skates.

The next day they all went out again. By Sunday afternoon Scott had learned to grind the bar and to do the spread eagle and a rink stop. And Mindy could slide along on her skates by herself.

"This is great!" Scott said. "I wish we could do it every day."

"You can go tomorrow after school," Mrs. Benson said. "But take Mindy with you while I do some shopping."

Scott groaned. He didn't want his little kindergarten sister around while he showed off the tricks he had learned. But Mindy was looking expectant. "Oh, all right," he said at last.

After school the next day Scott and Mindy rode home together on the school bus. They were sitting near the driver. "We're going ice skating," Mindy said. "My skates are new."

The bus driver glanced at them in the rearview mirror. "You kids are lucky, living out here in the country. When I was a kid I had to skate in a city rink. I went skating on a lake just once. The kids were playing crack-the-whip, and I was on the end. The kid next to me let go my hand and I went sailing into some bramble bushes growing at the edge. That didn't tickle."

"There aren't any bramble bushes at our pond," said Mindy, "but we've got polar bears."

"Is that right?" The bus driver winked at Scott. "Have fun," he called, as the children left the bus, "and take care."

When they were home, Scott went to the kitchen while Mrs. Benson helped Mindy into her snowsuit. Scott gulped down a glass of milk and ate two cookies. Then he ran and got his skates.

"Take good care of Mindy now," Mrs. Benson said as he was leaving the house with his sister. Scott sighed in disgust.

It had been snowing, but it had almost stopped by the time they reached the edge of the pond. Just a few flakes were whirling around in the wind. They sat on the bank to put on their skates. Scott fastened the double runners over Mindy's shoes, then put on his own skates and laced them up. Not far away the bigger boys had started a game of hockey. Scott skated over to watch, with Mindy stumbling along behind him.

After a few minutes one of the players offered Scott his stick. "Want to take my place a minute? I've got to go home for some gloves."

"You bet!" said Scott. "Thanks. You keep out of my way now, Mindy," he said to his sister.

17

Mindy nodded and stood far back, keeping out of the way of the flashing blades and swinging hockey sticks. But it was boring just standing there. She decided to find a stick for herself. She found a short branch near the shore and started looking for something to use as a puck. Just then the big white dog Scott had seen a few days before came running along and grabbed the stick.

"Hey!" cried Mindy. "You're a bad bear."

The dog ran over the ice, expecting Mindy to chase him. When Mindy stayed where she was, the dog dropped the stick and ran back to her. He barked and began biting playfully at her mitten. "Stop it!" said Mindy. Just then the dog saw something moving through the trees and went running off.

Scott, meanwhile, was in the middle of the hockey game. He came racing after the puck ahead of the others. His skate hit the stick and he went crashing down. And when he looked up, there was Mindy, reaching for the stick.

"That's my hockey stick," she said.

"Oh, Mindy!" Scott yelled. "That's a stupid thing to do! A person could get hurt that way. Don't you know any better than to leave sticks around on the ice?"

"I didn't," said Mindy. "The polar bear did it."

"Yeah, sure," Scott grumbled, brushing the snow from his knees.

By this time the other boy had come back with his gloves and Scott had no more chance to play. On the other side of the pond the boys his age were skating more slowly. Most of them had just learned to skate this year.

"Come on," Scott said to his sister. "I want to show them the tricks I learned."

They skated over toward his classmates. "Hey, George, Andy, Sharon—watch this!"

Scott ground the bar to the left and then to the right. He did the spread eagle and a rink stop. "Now watch this!" he said. He started to skate backward, and crashed right into Mindy. His friends all laughed.

"Now look what you did!" he said, helping her up. "Don't you know enough to keep out of the way? Go over there and skate by the bank."

"OK," said Mindy, and went sliding along, pretending to skate. When she was tired she went toward the shore and sat down to rest on a fallen log. After a moment the big white dog trotted over again and stood wagging his long tail.

"Here, bear," said Mindy, and patted his back. The dog stood still for a moment, but then someone whistled, and he was gone.

Scott was having a fine time lording it over his friends and teaching them the tricks he had learned. After a while he remembered Mindy and looked around for her. He saw her sitting on the log and skated over to her.

"Come on," he said. "We're going over there by the boathouse. You'll get cold sitting here all alone. Don't you remember what Daddy said? 'Stick with the others! Don't go off alone!'"

"But you told me to keep out of the way," Mindy said. "And anyway, I wasn't alone. I was patting the polar bear."

"Oh, sure," Scott said. "Look, Mindy, I'll give you one good ride and then you'll be on your own, OK?" They went back for Mindy's sled. "Hold on tight!" Scott said. He spun the sled around by its rope. Mindy shouted with excitement. "There," Scott said. "Now we're going to the boathouse. Come on along." And he skated off.

Near the boathouse the boys had started a game of tag, and Scott joined in. They chased each other back and forth, then stopped to pelt each other with snow. Soon it was getting dark. Suddenly Scott remembered Mindy.

The little girl was nowhere in sight. Scott wondered if she had gone home, but he didn't dare go and ask. If Mindy wasn't there, his mother would be worried. He skated to the bank near their house. There were two sets of footprints in the snow—the ones he and Mindy had made coming down to the pond. If Mindy had gone home, there would be another set.

Scott began to get frightened. He skated over to the hockey players. Only a few boys were left. "Anybody seen a little girl in a blue snowsuit?" he asked. No one had seen Mindy. Scott went back toward the boathouse. "Anybody seen my sister?" None of these boys and girls had seen Mindy, either.

Everyone was leaving the pond now. Scott sped through the crowd of boys and girls and across the pond, hoping to spot a blue snowsuit. It was still partly light. But all he could see in the distance was the big white dog, bounding into the trees with something in his mouth.

Scott was shaking. "Mindy! Mindy!" His voice echoed back from the hills. There was no place the little girl could be.

Then Scott remembered the cove. It was out of sight beyond a wooded hill called The Point. No one skated there, and no one swam there in the summer, either. It was mostly used for fishing. In fact, Scott suddenly remembered, some men had gone ice fishing at the cove last year, cutting holes in the ice. He did not want to think what might have happened if Mindy had wandered over there. With his heart pounding, Scott skated past The Point and turned toward the cove.

Sure enough, some holes had been cut in the ice. A sawhorse stood in front of the holes bearing a sign: DANGER. Scott's heart stood absolutely still, for he knew Mindy couldn't read yet. His eyes filled with tears. "Mindy!" he sobbed.

Then he heard a small voice call to him from the far side of a low dock. "Hey, Scott. Come see the fish."

It was Mindy's voice. Scott sped around the dock and found Mindy down on her hands and knees. She had scraped away the snow and was peering through the ice.

"Mindy! I told you to follow me to the boathouse!"

"Look," Mindy said. "I can see fish. They aren't frozen dead. I saw one wiggle."

Scott did not want her to know how frightened he had been. "Come on," he said. "It's time to go home."

Back on the bank near their own house Mrs. Benson was waiting. "It's late. I was getting worried," she said.

Scott said it wasn't his fault. "I had to go looking for Mindy. I told her to stick with us." He unlaced his skates and put on one cold shoe. That was all there was—one. He hopped around on one foot, searching around the bank.

Mrs. Benson had taken off Mindy's double runners. "Where's your other shoe, Scott? Did you lose it?"

"The polar bear took it," Mindy said. "I told Scott to watch out for him."

Scott suddenly remembered having seen the big white dog carrying something. He should have known better. Dogs sometimes did run off with your shoes and chew them. He should have put them in the fork of a tree.

"You're not so dumb at that, Mindy," he admitted.

Mrs. Benson said she would call the new neighbors on the telephone about the missing shoe. It gave her a good chance to get acquainted. "Come on, children," she said. "It's time for supper."

"Scott's smart," Mindy said as they trudged up the hill, Scott still hopping on one foot. "He can play hockey and do tricks. But I'm smart too. I know about polar bears."

WHAT WOULD YOU DO?

1. The ice has frozen, and you and your friends want to skate. You would
   - (a) throw a big rock on the ice to see if it holds.
   - (b) cut a hole in the ice near the shore and measure it to see if it is over three inches.
   - (c) walk out on the ice slowly, provided it has been freezing at least three days.

2. You are skating, and you see a dark spot ahead on the ice. You would
   - (a) skate over it.
   - (b) test it by hitting it with a branch.
   - (c) avoid that area.

3. You have decided to go skating, but find no one there. You would
   - (a) go ahead, since the ice was all right for skating that morning.
   - (b) go home.
   - (c) measure thickness of ice, then go ahead.

4. You are skating in a city rink, and you notice some older skaters doing tricks. You would
   - (a) keep away from that area.
   - (b) skate over and try out the tricks you learned yesterday.
   - (c) skate in that area but don't try any tricks.

5. You are in a race, and you want to avoid falling. You would

   (a) skate with shoulders back and knees bent.

   (b) skate leaning forward with knees bent.

   (c) skate leaning forward with knees straight.

6. You are skating in a city rink with a friend, and he falls behind. You would

   (a) turn around and go back to find him.

   (b) stay where you are and wait for him to catch up.

   (c) skate off to the side and wait for him to catch up.

TURN UPSIDE DOWN FOR ANSWERS.

ANSWERS

1. b This is the only sure way to tell thickness of ice. Never throw rocks or anything that will trip skaters onto the ice.

2. c Dark spots always mean thin ice.

3. b Never skate alone.

4. a You might get knocked down, and you will certainly get in the way of the expert skaters.

5. b This way you can catch yourself if you start to fall.

6. c People skate in one direction in a city rink. Never skate in reverse or stand still.